Buffy

THE
VAMPIRE SLAYER™

The
Remaining
Sunlight

Buffy THE VAMPIRE SLAYER™
The Remaining Sunlight

based on the television series created by JOSS WHEDON

writer ANDI WATSON   penciller JOE BENNETT

inker RICK KETCHAM

letterer JANICE CHIANG   photo cover artist DAVE STEWART

colorist GUY MAJOR

and featuring "MacGuffins"

writer J. L. VAN METER   penciller LUKE ROSS

inker RICK KETCHAM

colorist GUY MAJOR   letterer STEVE DUTRO

TITAN BOOKS

designer
KRISTEN BURDA

editors
SCOTT ALLIE AND BEN ABERNATHY

publisher
MIKE RICHARDSON

special thanks to
DEBBIE OLSHAN AT FOX LICENSING,
CAROLINE KALLAS AND GEORGE SNYDER AT *BUFFY THE VAMPIRE SLAYER*
AND DAVID CAMPITI AT GLASS HOUSE GRAPHICS.

PUBLISHED BY
TITAN BOOKS LTD.
42-44 DOLBEN STREET
LONDON SE1 0UP

FIRST EDITION: APRIL 1999
ISBN: 1-84023-078-9

3 5 7 9 10 8 6 4

printed in Italy by Valprint

Art by Arthur Adams; colors by Dave Stewart

WU-TANG FANG

SHE ALONE WILL STAND AGAINST THE VAMPIRES...

...THE DEMONS...

...AND THE FORCES OF DARKNESS.

SHE IS...

...THE SLAYER.

HI, GUYS.

THUMPA THUMPA

BRONZE CLUB

¡HEE HEE!

YEAH, RIGHT.

¡HAR HAR!

Ahh, IT'S SO NICE NOT TO BE KNEE DEEP IN GRAVEYARD DIRT WITH THE STENCH OF DECAYING YUCKY STUFF IN MY NOSTRILS.

YOU'VE NEVER BEEN IN THE BRONZE'S TOILETS, huh?

GURGLE

WAS THAT YOUR STOMACH?

I DON'T THINK SO.

GRAAAA!

WAAAAH!

¡Urghhh.¿

BUFFY!

WHO DIED?

HOW DID YOU KNOW THERE HAD BEEN A MURDER?

D'UH! WE'RE THE SCHOOL ON TOP OF THE HELLMOUTH. WE HAVE MORE DEATHS THAN FIRE DRILLS!

REALLY, BUFFY. THIS IS NO TIME FOR FLIPPANCY. LLOYD MODANO, THE SCHOOL KARATE CHAMPION, WAS FOUND DEAD ON THE SCHOOL GROUNDS THIS MORNING. IT APPEARS HE WAS KILLED AFTER SUPERVISING A LESSON YESTERDAY EVENING.

LLOYD? WHAT ENEMIES WOULD HE POSSIBLY HAVE?

THE BLOODSUCKING KIND. THE CARETAKER WHO FOUND HIM NOTICED TWO MARKS "LIKE HICKEYS" ON LLOYD'S NECK.

NOT ONLY THAT, BUT IT SEEMS LIKE HE HAD BEEN IN SOME FORM OF MARTIAL FIGHT. HE WAS BAREFOOT AND HAD LESIONS ALL OVER HIS BODY.

...SOMEWHAT LIKE XANDER'S FACE.

HEY, I DIDN'T KILL ANYONE. UH, A BOOKCASE FELL ON ME.

IF YOU KEEP INSISTING ON REACHING FOR THE TOP-SHELF MATERIAL...

YOU'RE GETTING OUR ROLES ALL MIXED UP HERE. I PUN, YOU FIGHT.

YES, BUT IF WE COULD KEEP OUR ATTENTION ON THE PROBLEM AT HAND.

DON'T YOU THINK IT'S ABOUT TIME YOU TOLD GILES ABOUT THE OTHER NIGHT, BUFFY?

WHAT OTHER NIGHT?

ANYWAY, NEWS FLASH. ISN'T BUFFY THE RESIDENT KUNG-PAO EXPERT? SHE'LL TRAIN YOU.

I'M TRYING TO AVOID BEING HUMILIATED BY PEOPLE I KNOW.

SO YOU'D RATHER BE HUMILIATED BY TOTAL STRANGERS?

EXACTLY! NOW STEP ASIDE, I HAVE ANOTHER LESSON TONIGHT.

I HAVE CONCEALER FOR YOUR EYE. IT'S JUST YOUR COLOR!

SURE, WEAR MAKE-UP TO KARATE CLASS. AND YET, I'M TRYING TO AVOID BEING BEATEN UP.

ISN'T THIS ALL A LITTLE, Y'KNOW?

WHEN I TELL YOU TO FIGHT, FIGHT!

WAH?!

UNDERSTAND, CANDY-BOY?

URRRKK!

YOU'LL LEARN TO DIE WITH HONOR.

Pencils by Chris Bachalo;
inks by Tim Townsend; *colors by* Liquid!

HALLOWEEN

Art by JOE BENNETT; colors by GUY MAJOR

COLD TURKEY

MacGUFFINS

WHAT'S IT *DO*?

ANYTHING IT *WANTS*, TECHNICALLY. IT'S NOT VERY STABLE.

IS THIS A *GOOD* IDEA? CAN'T IT WAIT?

NO, IT *CAN'T* WAIT.

"THE SLAYER'S GUARD IS DOWN *NOW*...

HI, *JUST-SAY-NO-TO-BUGS*? BUFFY SUMMERS. YOU GUYS ARE OVER AN HOUR LATE—

THAK

YAH! NO, NOT YOU. ABOUT THE YAH...

"...SHE'S OUT OF *PRACTICE*...

"...SHE WON'T BE *EXPECTING* A THREAT."

NOT COMING? *NOT* AN OPTION.

YEAH. THE *RAIN* RUINING MY DAY, TOO. YOU HEARD OF *PESTILENCE*?

BREACH OF CONTRACT? HAVE YOU HEARD OF THAT?

SNOT

Buffy THE VAMPIRE SLAYER
MACGUFFINS

"ER, UM. THEY'RE DESIGNED TO BE A *CHALLENGE,* BUFFY. WOULDN'T *DO* TO SIMPLY TELL YOU THE SOLUTION, ':*KOFF KOFF*:'"

OOH! YOU CAN PLAY MUSIC ON IT!

DEET DOOT BEEP

AND YOU'VE GOTTEN ME *FULLY* GROUNDED-- *AGAIN*--AND MY FATHER'S HOUSE IS MASTICATED.

OH, DEAR.

"ALL PART OF A GRAND *TRADITION,*" HE SAYS. 'CUZ YOU *KNOW* A GIRL WITH HER VERY OWN HELLMOUTH NEEDS TO FEEL SPECIAL.'

HEY, YO-- WATCH IT UP THERE! DON'T FALL ON ME!

BLAT BLAT BLAT BLAT

AND MY VACATION GETS *SANDBAGGED* BECAUSE YOU THINK I'LL SLACK! YOU REALLY DON'T TRUST ME TO *GIVE A DAMN,* DO YOU?

I SUPPOSE I COULD JUST *TELL* HER.

JUST *ONCE* HE COULD HAVE A LITTLE FAITH.

LITTLE HELP HERE?

BUSY...

BZZT!
BZZT!
BZZT!

HEY!
HEY!
HEY!

TIINK
TIINK

CAN'T BE HURT...

YO, PRINCESS! GIMME A HAND OVER HERE!

...PUZZLE TO MAKING THEM PASSIVE.

WAIT A MINUTE...

"WATCH IT. YA ALMOST HIT ME..."

"DON'T FALL ON ME..."

HEY!

UH-OH.

BONK

HAH!

JUST DOING OUR JOB, DEAR LADY.

ER, WHAT *TIME* IS IT?

'BOUT FOUR-THIRTY. YOU TWO START UP AGAIN WHEN?

GRACIOUS NO! YOU SOLVED THE PUZZLE. IT'S DONE.

SO I DID GOOD?

FORTY-SIX HOURS *FASTER* THAN THE SLAYER GARNHULD IN A.D. 562.

WATCHER BETTER NOT WEASEL OUT OF THE BET.

GILES *BET* ON ME?

SURE, HE WAS PRETTY CONFIDENT YOU COULD BEAT GARNHULD'S RECORD BY TWO FULL DAYS—YOU FIGURE HE'S GOOD FOR IT?

OH.

AWW. DON'T CRY— YOU ONLY MISSED IT BY TWO HOURS.